What are the Cows Thinking?

Written by Jeanne Gaugler
Illustrated by Valerie Bouthyette

What are the Cows Thinking

ISBN: 987-1-7354979-0-7
ISBN: 987-1-7354929-1-4

Requests for speaking events, extra book copies or permissions should be addressed to: jeannegaugler@gmail.com Published by Jeanne Gaugler
.

Printed in the United States of America

Sending my love to:

Carson, Finley, Brody, and Raegan,

Keep questioning, exploring, learning, and reading.

Fini was going to Grammy and Grampy's house
in the country for the first time!
She was so excited. Mommy had told her they
had animals on their farm, and Fini had questions.
A lot of questions. Especially about cows.

"Mommy, can cows see in the dark?" Fini asked.
"I'm not sure," Mom said, "but I bet Grammy will know."

"Do cows sleep standing up?" she asked.
Mom shook her head. "You'll have to ask Grammy."

Fini fidgeted in her seat. It was taking so long
to get to Grammy's farm!

Then, just as she was about to ask another question,
the car came to a stop.

"There's Grammy!" Fini blurted excitedly.
Fini scrambled out of the car.

"Grammy, I want to see the cows!" she shouted.
Grammy laughed. "Well then, that is just what we'll do."

Taking Fini by the hand, Grammy led her across the field.
As they got closer to the fence, Fini asked,
"Grammy, why are the cows staring at us?"

"Well Fin Bear, they've never seen you before. You are a
stranger to them. Cows get nervous when a stranger is nearby."

Fini gazed at the cows in wonder.
"Which cows are girls?" she asked.

"Well, Fin Bear, all of the cows are female," she
said. "A male is called a bull. We don't have
any bulls on our farm."

Grammy picked Fini up so she could climb onto the
fence for a better view of the cows.

"Do they only eat hay?" Fini asked, pointing
to a large hay bale.

"Mostly," Grammy replied. "When the grass grows
high in the pasture, Grampy opens the gate so the
cows can eat green grass."

Fini jumped off the fence and sprinted down the field.

"Where are you going, Fin Bear?" Grammy shouted.

"I want to get closer to that cow that is mooing and looking over the fence. I think something is wrong," Fini desperately bellowed.

Grammy caught up to Fini and took her hand.
"Running by the fence can make the cows nervous,
especially the one who is mooing," Grammy explained.

"Why?" Fini asked.
Grammy led Fini farther out into the field and
pointed at the tall grass. "Do you see it?" she asked.

"Oh, Grammy, it is a baby!" Fini declared in amazement.

"It sure is, Fin Bear. The calf easily scooted under the fence, but the mama cow can't fit. She's nervous because her baby is too far away. That's why she's mooing so loudly. Come on. Let's help the baby calf get under the fence so mama cow can relax."

Fini watched the calf run to her mama.
"Yuck, why is the mama cow licking her baby?" she asked.

"That is the sign of a good mama," Grammy explained.
"Your family gives hugs to show they care.
Cows bond with their babies by licking them."

"Do you think the cows can hear what we are saying Grammy?" Fini whispered.

Grammy whispered back, "They may not understand what you are talking about, but they hear your voice."

"Look, Grampy is getting ready to feed the cows!
I'm so happy I get to see it!"
Fini shivered with excitement, and then paused.
"Grammy? Will the cows bite me?"

"No, they can't bite you because they don't
have top front teeth," Grammy said.

"So the cows can't hurt me?
Then can I go inside the fence with Grampy?" Fini asked.

"I never said they can't hurt you!" Grammy said.
"If cows are scared or feel threatened, they could charge at you.
Especially the mama cows. They'll do anything to protect
their babies—even chase you.
That's why we stay outside the fence."

"Then why does Grampy go inside the fence?" Fini asked.

"Grampy feeds the cows every day and makes sure their
water bowls are always working properly.
They trust him because he takes care of them,
but Grampy is cautious. He knows a cow could
hurt him if he is not careful."

Fini sat for a minute, watching the cows.
"What are the cows thinking, Grammy?" she asked at last.

"That is a very good question, Fin Bear.
They probably think about eating and drinking.
If they have a calf, they think
about keeping it safe," Grammy replied.

Just then, Fini let out a big yawn.
Grammy smiled and put an arm around her.
"I think it's time to say good night to the cows, Fin Bear.
Let's go inside and find a good book to read before bedtime."

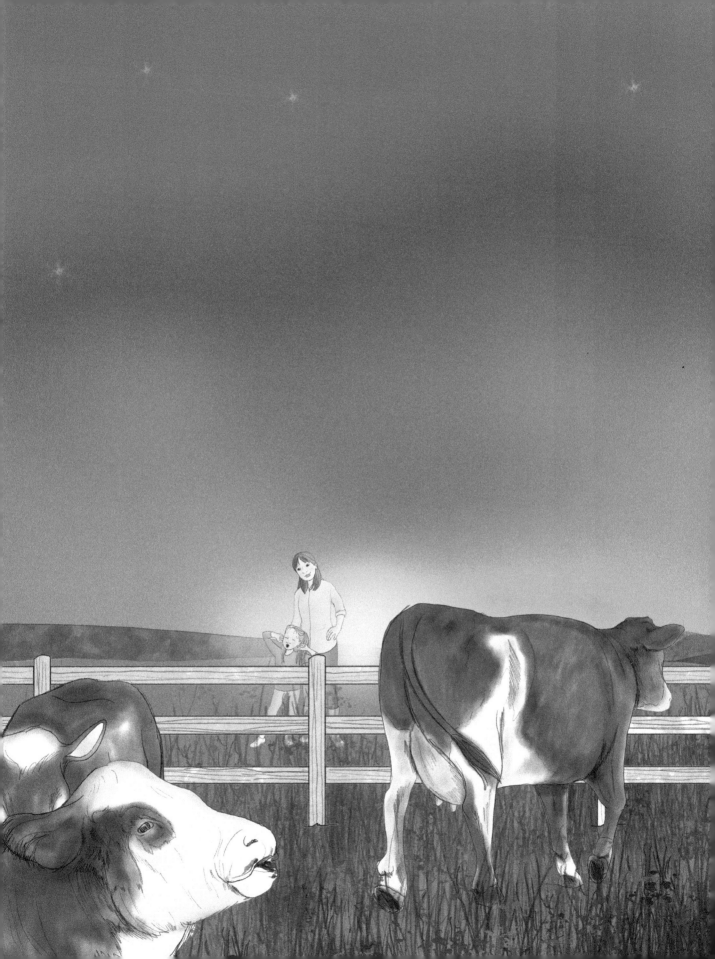

"Do you have a book about cows?" Fini asked excitedly.
"I'm sure I can find one, Fin Bear." Grammy said
with a smile. "Let's go see."

CPSIA information can be obtained
at www.ICGtesting.com
Printed in the USA
LVHW070354250920
667082LV00037B/495